SATURDAY MARKET

PATRICIA GROSSMAN ✳ **ENRIQUE O. SÁNCHEZ**

LOTHROP, LEE & SHEPARD BOOKS

NEW YORK

By FRIDAY NIGHT, EVERYONE IS READY. The ones from far
away load their trucks and carts and donkeys. They travel
by moonlight. Estela and Ana live closer to the market, so
they can sleep through most of the moonlit night. But
everyone—the ones from far and the ones from near—
arrives at the market before dawn. They will work all day,
selling their wares first to a few people, then to many.

LAST WEEK MIGUEL SOLD ten sacks of chile peppers. Eight different kinds. This week he brought more. *Mexicanos* take Miguel's chiles home to make hot sauce. *Turistas* from up north jump when they taste the fiery hot chiles. Their tongues glow red, but they buy, too.

CARMEN SOLD ONLY TWO *REBOZOS* LAST WEEK. Women always need *rebozos*, the beautiful shawls that warm their shoulders or shield their babies from the noonday sun. But so many women sell *rebozos* at market! María and Margarita and Elena. One day, worries Carmen, there will be more *rebozo* sellers than women to buy their wares.

LUIS HAS RAISED HIS FIRST PIG, and it is fat and charming. He has dressed it in a fine sash to make it beautiful for market, but secretly he hopes no one will buy his pig. In his heart, Luis cannot bear to think that his fat and charming pig will become a rich man's feast.

Each week Rosa brings two hundred pairs of *huaraches* to market. Everyone wears *huaraches*—to work in the fields, to feed the roosters, to dance in the *zócalo*. But Rosa must have leather to make her *huaraches*, and this week the Monday delivery of leather did not come until Wednesday. Rosa had to stitch like a *loca* woman. She had to stitch like never before, but she made it—two hundred pairs of *huaraches*, just as usual.

SATURDAY MARKET

To Wolfie—P.G.

To my wife Joan—E.O.S.

The illustrations in this book were done in acrlylic paints on canvas. The display type was set in Jazz. The text was set in
Goudy Sans. Printed and bound by South China. Production supervision by Esilda Martinez. Designed by Robin Ballard.

PEDRO'S FAMILY HAS WOVEN some fine rugs, and Pedro has brought them to market. Their designs enchant him. They are the ancient designs of the Mayan people, and each tells a story from long ago. At market, Pedro tells the story of each rug. Maybe someone buys a rug; maybe someone just tells the story of the rug to another person. But each *turista* who stops at Pedro's stall learns something new about the ancient Maya.

DURING THE WEEK, ESTELA SITS with her flowers in the
zócalo. People are often too busy to buy. So Estela comes
to the big Saturday market. Here, everyone watches her
tie her calla lilies into bunches. She ties them with bright
red rope, but she makes sure that each blossom breathes
the open air. Then people buy. All through the night,
sweethearts will bring Estela's flowers to each other.

LAST SATURDAY AT MARKET, PACO BOUGHT a rooster that does not crow. This week, he slept so late that his chickens lost their voices squawking to be fed, his goats came to his window bleating to be milked, and the sky fell dark before Paco had finished plowing his field. All because a cheat sold Paco a rooster that does not crow. *This* Saturday, Paco has returned to market. He plans to give back the silent rooster and make the cheat give him *two* roosters that crow.

 EACH SATURDAY, LUCÍA SITS with her potions, her good
luck pieces, and her voodoo dolls. Lucía is the charm
lady. Maybe this week she'll sell a magic ring to a farmer
so his fields will grow the sweetest corn. Or maybe she'll
cast a spell on the cheat who sells people roosters that
do not crow. But whatever she sells, she will do a fine
business. People come to buy their friends good luck.
They come to buy their enemies bad luck.

THE BREADS JUAN HAS BAKED are crusty rings and huge, doughy swirls. Some of his cookies are flat, and some are puffy and round and laced with coconut. Sometimes Juan snitches a cookie, but for each one he takes, he drops a *nuevo peso* into his pocket. By the time he leaves the market, Juan will have a full stomach and a full pocket, but he will drive away in an empty truck.

ANA HAS SET HER *TORTILLA* STAND at the edge of the
market. She sings as she mixes cornmeal with lime,
squirts on water, rolls the balls, pats them flat, and cooks
them. People are in a hurry when they enter the market.
They don't always stop to buy a *tortilla*. But everyone
looks back to smile in the direction of the good smell and
the sweet notes that fill the air.

DURING THE WEEK, PARROTS FLY all around Diego's courtyard. When they are not flying, they are climbing trees. Diego's favorite parrot, Carlos, has a green body, a red head, yellow wings, and a blue tail. At market, Carlos keeps Diego company all day. People offer to buy Carlos. Diego asks, "Would you sell your *mejor amigo*?" Then he points to the other lovely parrots. Some people walk away; others buy.

ENRIQUE SHAPES PEOPLE OUT OF CLAY—his own people, the *Zapotecas*. He makes them so small, he can fit a whole family on his palm. His men wear tiny bandannas, and his women wear tiny *rebozos*. Many *turistas* buy Enrique's Zapotec figurines. Way up north, they will place them on their desk tops or on their mantles.

By THE TIME PEOPLE REACH ANA, they have finished their
Saturday marketing. Now they stop to listen to Ana and
to show her their patterned rugs, their fragrant lilies,
and their roosters that crow. Ana cooks up more *tortillas*.
They show her herbs to cure their aches, breads to fill
their bellies, parrots to brighten their courtyards, tiny clay
Zapotec figurines to stand on their palms. Sometimes
they hug Ana. Maybe they invite her to join them at the
market next Saturday, to sample some chile peppers, to
buy herself a new *rebozo*. No, says Ana. She will be busy
from dawn to dusk, serving *tortillas* to a market as full
as the world.

GLOSSARY OF SPANISH WORDS

amigo/amiga (ah-MEE-goh/ah-MEE-gah): friend, comrade

huaraches (also guaraches) (huah-RAH-chays): Mexican leather sandals

loco/loca (LOH-koh/LOH-kah): crazy

mejor (MAY-hor): best

Mexicano/Mexicana (may-he-KAH-noh/may-he-KAH-nah): native of Mexico

nuevo peso (noo-AY-voh PAY-soh): monetary coin of Mexico

rebozo (ray-BOH-zoh): shawl

tortilla (tor-TEE-yah): thin pancake made of corn or wheat flour

turista (too-REES-tah): tourist, traveler

zócalo (ZOH-kah-loh): public square

Zapotecas (zah-poh-TAY-kahs): Zapotec people

(**NOTE**: Where alternative endings to words are given, the "o" ending indicates male, the "a" ending indicates female.)